D0714208

Opal

The Monstrous Forest

Opal

The Monstrous Forest

Rose Lacey

Willow
Tree

A CIP catalogue record for this book is
available from the British Library

Published by Willow Tree Books, 2019
Willow Tree Books, Tide Mill Way, Woodbridge, Suffolk, IP12 1AP

0 2 4 6 8 9 7 5 3 1

Series concept © 2019 Willow Tree Books
Text © 2019 Working Partners Limited
London, WC1X 9HH
Cover illustration © 2019 Willow Tree Books
Interior illustrations © 2019 Willow Tree Books

Special thanks to Lil Chase

Willow Tree Books, Princess Pirates and associated logos are
trademarks and/or registered trademarks of Imagine That Group Ltd

ISBN: 978-1-78700-734-5
Printed and bound in Great Britain
by Bell and Bain Ltd, Glasgow

www.willowtreebooks.net

For my son, Robert

Prologue

Many years have passed, but the memory
of the royal infant and the panther cub is still
fresh. Thunder was the panther's name, and I –
Celestine the seawitch – watched alongside the
child's parents as he climbed into the basket we
had placed her in. The tiny baby cooed as the cub
turned around three times then dropped down
next to her, purring.

"You see," I told the king and queen, "even so
young, they are perfect companions."

Two adult panthers sat at the feet of the king

and queen. The queen smiled and fastened a golden locket around the cub's neck and then placed a gold ring, with a circular purple stone, in the basket. Her face furrowed with sadness.

"Even Thunder cannot protect Opal from what is about to happen," she said.

I sighed. The queen was right: Obsidian was closing in on us. I had to get the five royal families on to their ship, and I had to get the five royal princesses as far away as possible.

The baby put her hand on the panther's head and giggled, her amber eyes sparkling. Her hair was as dark as the panther's fur. The cub closed his yellow eyes. The separation would be hard on them both.

"My Opal," said the queen, bending down to kiss the child's forehead, her long braids falling past her shoulder as she did. The king lifted Thunder and placed the cub beside his parents. Then he picked up the basket and we hurried to board the ship, in the faint hope that we would all survive Obsidian's attack.

But it was not to be.

Though the princesses escaped, drifting out to sea and off to another world, their parents did not. The panther cub lived, only to be captured by the wicked Obsidian.

It is Princess Opal and Thunder's destiny to reunite, find the magical Treasure of the Purple Isle, and save Lemuria. And the reunion can't come soon enough. Opal's island is in dire need of her help. It will take courage to stand up to

Obsidian after all these years.

   But I see great courage in Opal.

   Now she must find it in herself.

Chapter 1

A microphone screeched. Three zookeepers stepped up on to a little ledge in front of the otter pool. Two of the zookeepers carried buckets, and they began throwing fish into the water. The little otter family swam over and gobbled up the food.

"I'd love to feed the otters," Opal breathed.

"You'd make a brilliant zookeeper," Topaz told her. "You know, if you could fit it in around all your princessing and pirating duties."

Opal and her friends – Topaz, Coral, Pearl and Jade – all giggled. Here, they were normal schoolgirls. But in the Kingdom of Lemuria, they were princesses with an awesome pirate ship.

"Hello everyone," called the youngest zookeeper with the microphone. She was a short girl with a cropped bob, probably not that much older than them. She seemed so calm speaking into the microphone in front of all these people. Opal wished she had that kind of confidence.

"We're going to do a quiz," the zookeeper said. "And if you get a question right, you get to feed the otters!"

Opal's four friends looked at her. "You're about to get your wish," whispered Pearl, jumping up and down, making her blonde pigtails bob.

Opal bit her lip. "I have to get the question right first," she frowned.

"Question one," the young zookeeper said. "How many different types of otter do we have here at our zoo?"

That was easy: there were two, it said so on the sign in front of them. Coral nudged Opal to say something.

Kate from the year above didn't wait to be asked before calling out, "Two. Lontra otters and Lutra otters." Opal watched with envy as Kate climbed up and grabbed a handful of fish, throwing it to the otters.

"Question two," said the zookeeper. "What do otters carry with them to open clam shells?"

Coral nudged Opal again and grinned her friendly grin.

Jade nodded encouragingly.

"Go on, Opal," said Pearl.

Topaz grabbed Opal's hand and thrust it in the air. "Opal knows!" she yelled.

Everyone turned to look at Opal. Her heart raced. She knew she knew the answer, and she *really* wanted to feed the cute little otters. She opened her mouth … but nothing came out.

The microphone screeched again, cutting through the silence like a police siren.

A couple of the older Breakwater girls sniggered.

They're laughing at me, Opal thought. Her face was getting hot. Feeling like she was suffocating in the cool November air, Opal turned and ran, pushing past her friends and the other girls, running until she saw a sign for the toilet. She dashed inside, got into the nearest cubicle and locked the door behind her.

That was so embarrassing! This happened every time Opal needed to speak in front of people. She knew it would be less embarrassing to just talk, rather than run away and cause a scene, but the words stuck in her throat.

Seconds later she heard the outside door open and four pairs of feet rush in.

"Opal!" called Coral.

"Are you in here?" asked Jade.

"Are you OK?" asked Pearl.

There was a soft tap on the door of her cubicle. "Opal, I'm so sorry," said Topaz, "I didn't mean to put you on the spot like that."

Opal took a deep breath and pulled herself together. Topaz shouldn't feel bad. She had only tried to help because she knew how much Opal wanted to feed the animals. Opal opened the door and Topaz instantly wrapped her in a hug.

"Am I the worst friend ever?"

Opal laughed. "Of course not. You were only—"

A gasp from Pearl made Opal pull away from Topaz. The others were looking at their rings.

They were glowing!

"You know what this means, girls," Opal said, her anxiety instantly replaced with excitement.

"We're off to Lemuria!" they all chorused together.

"I can't wait to see Nestor," said Opal. Their three-masted pirate ship had a talking figurehead

shaped like a horse. He was always grumpy, but
they knew he loved them.

"I wonder what trouble Jasper's in this time,"
said Jade. Jasper was their friend in Lemuria.
His imprisoned parents had made the map that
showed where each of the magical Treasures
were hidden. They had to get the Treasures
before Obsidian did, otherwise she'd control the
islands and be able to rule Lemuria.

"Come on, girls," said Topaz, pushing back
her thick auburn hair. "Ring bump."

Topaz brought her fist forward and the other
girls did the same. Opal's ring stone was a flat
circle, purple with flecks of every colour in it.
Looking at it was like looking into the whole
universe – the multicoloured flecks like stars in a
purple night sky.

"All friends on deck!" they called together,
which felt like a funny thing to say in a public

toilet. But as
soon as their
rings made
contact, there
was a flash of
golden light, so
bright it made
Opal squeeze
her eyes shut.

She wasn't scared: this was exactly what
happened every time they'd travelled to Lemuria.
And each time they'd arrived safely on the deck
of their beloved Nestor.

Before she even opened her eyes, Opal could
feel the warmth of the sun and hear the sounds
of the sea all around her. "Nestor! We're here!"
she cried.

But when Opal finally opened her eyes, she
found that she and her friends weren't on the

wooden boards of their pirate ship at all. They stood on a tiny spit of sand in the middle of the ocean, with nothing around for miles!

"I hate to say it," said Topaz, "but I think we're marooned!"

Opal bit her lip and stared at the deep water all around them. *How could they get off this island?*

Chapter 2

A deep pool of dread welled up in Opal's stomach. They were on an island about the size of a school classroom, made of nothing but sand. There wasn't even a palm tree for shelter. From the frowns on her friends' faces she could tell they were just as worried as she was. They were all dressed in their princess pirate outfits now – but, where was their ship?

"Anyone got any bright ideas?" asked Pearl, tipping her head to one side.

Opal shaded her eyes with her hand and

looked around. There wasn't much to see, just ocean. But then she spotted a dark shape on the horizon.

"Is that ..." – she pointed the shape out to her friends – "another island?"

They all turned to look, then grinned at each other hopefully.

Pearl bounced up and down. "It *is* an island!" She began to wade into the water. "We can swim to it." Her legs were already shimmering like the sea that surrounded her, about to transform into a tail.

In Lemuria, the five friends had magical powers: Topaz was super strong, Coral could control the elements, Jade created amazing inventions, and Pearl could turn into a mermaid. Opal loved her own power: talking to animals!

Jade pulled Pearl back by the shoulder. "Correction," she said. "*You* can swim to it. I don't think any of the rest of us can make it that far."

Opal was about to suggest that Pearl could pull them all along when she felt her toes getting wet. She looked down to see waves lapping over her feet.

"Uh-oh," she said. "Look! The tide's coming in."

"If the tide gets much higher," said Topaz, with a frown, "the whole island will be underwater!"

"If only there was *anything* on this island I could use to make something," Jade said. She was wearing a tool belt she'd made after borrowing one on her own island. But even Jade would find it hard to make something out of just sand and seawater.

"I'll go," said Pearl, diving into the water, her legs fully transforming into a purple-green shimmering fishtail. "And I'll come right back. Maybe I'll find a raft or something."

Topaz nodded. "Go quickly."

"Aye aye, Captain," Pearl replied with a salute, before disappearing under the water.

Opal watched the waves in the distance, trying to spot her friend. The island was getting smaller and smaller as the tide rose. They didn't have long.

Finally, Pearl broke through the surface. She was grinning. "Opal!" she shouted.

Opal ran into the waves, not caring how wet her clothes were now.

Pearl swam closer, calling as she came. "I've just seen a pod of dolphins!"

Behind her, Coral clapped her hands in delight. "Dolphins!" she breathed.

"If I take you to them," Pearl said, "do you think you could ask them for help?"

"I'll try." Opal smiled nervously.

"You can do it, Opal," said Topaz.

"You're kind of our only hope," Jade pointed out.

Opal dived into the water and reached for Pearl's hand. Pearl grabbed her and began to pull her along. Opal took a deep breath and then they were gliding under the surface, faster than Opal had ever swum before.

When Pearl took her up to the surface so she could catch her breath, Opal gasped to see seven majestic dolphins leap through the air. The dolphins were chatting away happily, although

Opal wasn't close enough to make out what they were saying.

"Hello!" Opal called to them. She didn't feel nervous talking to animals like she did when she spoke to people.

The dolphins changed direction, and swam towards them. Pearl put an arm around Opal to help her stay above the water as the dolphins surrounded them. They looked friendly.

"Who are you?" asked one dolphin.

"I'm Princess Op—" Opal started.

"Why can this human talk to us?" interrupted one of the dolphins, his voice clicking as he spoke.

"Do you think she's a witch?" asked another.

"Oh no. I'm not—" said Opal.

"And who's this mermaid? We don't normally get mermaids in this part of the ocean."

"This is Princess Pearl. She—"

"Are they talking about me?" asked Pearl.

"Hel. Lo." she said slowly, turning to the dolphins.
"I. Am. Pearl."

"What's the mermaid saying?" asked a
dolphin with a grey-blue streak down his back.
"Humans usually have a boat. Don't you have a
boat?"

Opal shook her head. "That's the problem.
My friends and I were wondering if you'd take us
to that island over there, please." She pointed to
the island far away, in the distance.

The dolphins all backed away from them at
the same time, speaking nervously in turn.

"We want to help you."

"You seem like a nice human."

"But we won't go near that place."

"The Purple Isle is dangerous. We haven't
been close to it for many years."

Opal gasped. The Purple Isle was *her* island!
"What's happened to it?" she asked, scared to

hear the answer.

"The island is cursed," answered one dolphin.

"The animals have turned into monsters," said another.

Opal guessed the missing Treasure had something to do with this – it had affected the other islands they'd been to, each in different ways. "All the more reason to get there," Opal said.

The dolphins looked at each other as if deciding what to do. "We won't go to the island, but we saw a big ship passing recently," said a darker dolphin. "We could take you to it."

"Oh, thank you, thank you!" cried Opal.

"What did they say? Is something wrong?" Pearl asked. She hadn't understood a word.

"Yes, there's something wrong on the island," replied Opal, "but they'll take us to a ship nearby." Pearl grinned.

The dolphin with the grey-blue streak pulled Opal back to where their friends were waiting. The other dolphins came too, and Pearl swam along with them. Opal glanced back at the Purple Isle, far away in the distance. There was nothing she hated more than the thought of animals in danger.

The sandy spit of land Opal's friends were standing on was now about the size of her bed back at school.

"We've found a lift!" Pearl called to the others.

Topaz and Coral grinned and splashed into the waves. Jade was a little more cautious, but she came too. *I guess everyone wants to ride a dolphin, even someone who's scared of water!* Opal thought.

Each girl jumped on to a dolphin, and soon Opal was going even faster than she had with Pearl. Pearl was barely able to keep up. Opal

The Monstrous Forest

grinned at her friends, and even Jade smiled back.

"I bet the ship they saw was Nestor," said Coral, calling over the sound of the waves.

"At this speed we'll be there in no time!" Topaz said.

And Topaz was right. They rounded a large rock and there, in front of them, was a three-masted pirate ship. Topaz patted her dolphin on the back before sliding off and swimming towards the ship.

"Nestor!" she called. "It's us!" She began to scramble up a rope that dangled off the side.

"Nestor!" said Coral, following closely after Topaz. "Have you missed us? We sure have missed you."

Opal thanked her dolphin for the ride.

"Good luck!" he nickered in reply, then all of the dolphins swam off, waving their tails to the girls as they went.

Opal climbed up behind her friends. Hauling herself over the side, she dropped down on to the deck with a loud thump.

The next thing Opal heard was a muffled yelp. Then Topaz stumbled from behind the main mast in the centre of the deck, with someone's hand clamped over her mouth. Opal's heart sank.

Out stepped Obsidian, her black cape swirling around her in the breeze. Her bony fingers smothered Topaz's words.

"Hello princesses,"

she cackled. "I'm so glad you came!"

This wasn't Nestor – it was Obsidian's ship!
Opal stood side-by-side with Jade, Pearl and
Coral, watching in horror as Topaz struggled.

"How kind you are, little princesses,"
Obsidian said with a smile. The hair beneath
her crown didn't move, even in the sea breeze.
"You've delivered yourselves to me – all five of
you at once!"

Obsidian pushed Topaz forward. Topaz
tripped but quickly righted herself, then stepped
backwards on to Obsidian's foot!

"Arrrrgh!" Obsidian yowled, letting go of
Topaz.

"That was a super-strength stomp!" Topaz
announced with a grin. Opal couldn't help
wincing. Topaz's strength was her magical power,
and that would have hurt!

Obsidian hopped around the deck, holding on

to her foot. "Larry! Boil! Get them!" she shrieked.

Larry – tall and gangly with a pencil moustache – appeared from the captain's cabin. He raced forward with his sword drawn. Topaz

drew the cutlass that was tucked into her belt. She slashed and parried, swishing her cutlass and defending and blocking every stab from Larry's sword. The clash of metal on metal made Opal wince.

Boil waddled down the steps from the quarterdeck. A button popped off his waistcoat as he charged towards them like a bowling ball. Coral held out both of her arms in front of her. "Stop right there!" she yelled, using her magical power to blast Boil with a wind so strong that he fell on his bottom and slid all the way along the deck, back to the stairs he'd just run down.

Jade was holding a tool from her tool belt and fiddling with something in her hands.

"Pearl! Here!" she cried, throwing one end of what looked like a rope with some sort of mechanism on the end. Then she carried on fiddling with the other end.

Opal heard a blood-curdling growl, then Snarl and Menace – Obsidian's wolves – burst out from a trapdoor.

Opal stood in front of the wolves. "Stop right there!" she told them, trying to ignore the drool dripping from their lips as they circled her. "Come with us and we'll set you free."

"We're Obsidian's wolves," said Snarl.

"We do whatever Obsidian wants," said

Menace. Their tone was so flat that Opal knew they were under some kind of spell.

"Pearl – now!" shouted Jade, and together she and Pearl threw the device she had been working on. Opal had thought it was a rope, but as it unravelled she could see it was a net. It wrapped around Snarl and Menace, then closed so that the two wolves were trapped inside, yelping as they pushed against each other.

"Nice work, Jade!" Opal called.

Jade and Pearl were already hard at work on another device. Coral was holding Boil back, and Topaz was still battling Larry, while Obsidian hopped around on one foot. Opal felt a little helpless. Being able to talk to animals was a cool power to have ... but pretty useless when the only animals around were enchanted by Obsidian.

Just then, Opal heard a voice calling from the trapdoor Snarl and Menace had appeared from.

"Who's there? Can anyone help me?"

Opal realised that whoever was talking was an animal, not a person. She ran towards the voice.

Perhaps her power would come in useful after all!

Chapter 3

Opal dropped through the trapdoor of Obsidian's ship and landed in a dank, dark galley. "Hello?" she called.

"Over here!" the animal growled.

Opal picked her way through the ship, carefully stepping over the ropes and barrels strewn across the floor. Only small circles of light shone through the portholes at the side. Finally, the galley opened out and Opal saw a cage. Inside the cage shone two bright yellow eyes, looking directly at her.

"Don't worry," Opal said, her arm outstretched. "I'll get you out."

The animal's eyes widened and it stepped closer to the bars of the cage, into the light. Opal saw it was a sleek black panther. "Opal?" he said, quietly.

Opal frowned. "How do you—?"

"Opal!" the panther said more loudly, his ears pricked up as he paced back and forth, rubbing against the bars. "It's Thunder! But of course you don't remember me. You were so young. And I was just a cub!"

"You know me?" Opal asked in disbelief.

The panther stopped pacing and bowed low in front of Opal. "Princess Opal of the Purple Isle. We were born on the very same day. I was brought to the palace to be your companion."

Opal grinned. Her own panther! That was a pretty cool pet! "I'm so pleased to meet you,"

she said, wondering what Thunder could tell her about where she'd come from. "Tell me about the Purple Isle."

"It's a beautiful place," Thunder told her, "covered with trees and pools of clear water. Animals and people live happily together ..." Then Thunder hesitated. "Or, at least, they used to. Until the magical Treasure was hidden. Then the animals seemed to fall under a curse."

"What sort of curse?" asked Opal.

"Errr," mewed Thunder, flicking his tail. "How about we talk about this later?"

"Oh! Of course!" Opal said, spotting the key to Thunder's cage dangling from a hook. She jumped up to reach it, then unlocked the cage door.

"Now let's get that horrible witch," said Thunder, already bounding away.

"I'm right behind you," Opal cried.

They got to the hatch and peered out. The wolves were still trapped in the net. Topaz was battling Obsidian now – staff against cutlass. Coral was conjuring up wave after wave, splashing Boil every time he tried to get up. Meanwhile, Pearl and Jade were fighting Larry. Opal watched in horror as Pearl fell over, and Larry raised his sword over his head.

"Pearl!" Opal called out.

Thunder streaked across the deck and knocked Larry down. Larry hid behind his hands and howled with fear.

Obsidian yelped. "What's that mangy cat doing out of its cage?"

Topaz turned to look, and Obsidian took her opportunity: she shot a blast from her staff, throwing Topaz to the floor. Opal raced forward to defend her, but now Obsidian had them both in her sights.

"Ahoy, ahoy!" a voice squawked.

Opal looked up to see a parrot – red with blue-and-yellow markings – flapping overhead.

"Pegleg!" the girls called out together.

The parrot screeched, and Opal's heart lifted. "He says they've been looking for us!"

"They?" said Jade, spinning around.

Another three-masted pirate ship was sailing up beside Obsidian's.

"Nestor!" the girls called as loud as they could.

"Nooooo!" yelled Obsidian.

"Yessssss!" Pearl yelled back.

"Hello princesses," said Nestor, the regal

figurehead at the front of the ship. "I should have guessed you'd be in trouble somewhere."

"Good to see you too, Nestor," said Topaz.

Five ropes swung across the gap between the ships. "Catch!" shouted a boy's voice.

The five princesses grabbed the ropes as their friend Jasper popped up on Nestor's deck and waved.

"My turn to help you out of a scrape for a change!" he said with a grin.

"Are you coming, Thunder?" asked Opal.

"You bet," said the panther, and he took a running leap, easily clearing the gap between the boats.

The girls swung across to the safety of their own ship.

Obsidian screamed in frustration. "Useless!" she shouted at her henchmen. "Both of you. And you stupid wolves!" She shot another blast from her staff but it missed Nestor completely. "Get to the cannons! Sink that ship!" Obsidian shrieked.

"We need to get out of here fast," said Pearl.

"Girls," Topaz called out. "To your positions." She ran to the back of the ship and the quarterdeck where the ship's wheel was.

"Aye aye, Captain!" Opal shouted as she ran to the mainmast. Pearl hurried to the foremast, Coral to the mizzenmast and Jade to the telescope at the bow. Jasper climbed up the rigging to the crow's nest, and Pegleg flapped overhead.

"Coral," Topaz called over her shoulder. "If you could give us a little help getting away, that would be great."

"On it, Captain," Coral replied. She held out her arms and blew a gust of wind directly into Nestor's sails. Suddenly it was as though a gale was blowing just for them. The sails filled and they sped away from Obsidian's ship.

The Purple Isle grew closer and closer. Opal could see that it was covered in a huge forest. And in between some of the trees she could see a river – just wide enough for Nestor to sail down.

"There!" Opal cried out. "Head for that inlet."

"Our home," Thunder purred, beside her.

Opal felt a thrill of excitement. She would finally see where she was born. Her palace, her home. And though her family were long gone, she would no doubt find out more about them.

Opal

The Monstrous Forest

The ship changed direction and they headed into the inlet and up the river. Behind them, Obsidian's screams turned to cackles of laughter. "You've done my job for me! The Purple Isle will take care of you!" she called after them. "It's dealt with many of my enemies before."

Opal shuddered with fear. What would they find on the Purple Isle?

They cruised slowly down the river, tall trees and vines rising above them on both sides. Topaz walked back to the centre of the ship and called the others over.

"This is Thunder," Opal told her friends, pointing to the panther by her side.

"Aww, so cute," said Coral, stroking him behind the ears.

Thunder didn't seem to mind being called cute. He closed his eyes and leaned into Coral's ear-scratching.

Opal was about to tell the others that the animals here were under a curse, but she was interrupted by a shriek from the trees.

The girls looked around as the shriek grew louder and was joined by more angry-sounding squawks. Then something brightly coloured dived out of the trees straight at Nestor's sails.

"What's that?" cried Jade.

They were birds! They came one after another, diving at the ship, tearing holes in the sails.

"Stop!" cried Opal, trying to reason with the birds. "We've come to help!"

But Opal had to jump out of the way to avoid a coconut flying towards her. "Hey!" she cried, looking up to see a monkey snarling and throwing coconuts at them. Its eyes were a terrifying shade of blood-red.

"What's their problem?" asked Pearl, covering

her head with her arm. "What are they saying, Opal?"

"Opal!" Topaz yelled, as she took cover behind the mainmast. "Ask them to stop!"

Opal winced as she tried to decipher the terrifying noises coming from the animals. But she couldn't, not a word. "I don't understand," said Opal. "And, I don't understand why I don't understand!" Normally she could hear the words of every animal in Lemuria, as clearly as she could understand her friends.

Suddenly the birds and monkeys all looked up into the sky and flew, hopped or swung away from Nestor's deck, hooting and screeching.

Pegleg squawked in surprise, looking up, too.

"What is it, Pegleg?" asked Opal.

"Dad and Mum, Mum and Dad!" he squawked loudly.

Two red parrots with blue-and-yellow

markings swooped down towards them. They looked just like Pegleg, one with an eyepatch, the other with a wooden leg.

Jasper smiled, despite having to dodge another coconut attack. "If Pegleg's parents are here, then maybe my parents are here, too!" Opal had never seen him look happier. "Goldie! Loot!" Jasper called out to the parrots. "Have you seen my mum and dad?"

Goldie and Loot did not stop or change direction. They didn't fly towards Pegleg, who was hopping and squawking happily. Instead they headed for Jasper, landing on his backpack.

"Hey!" cried Jasper as the parrots pecked at him again and again. "What are you doing? Goldie?"

The bigger parrot – Goldie – didn't answer, but pushed his head into Jasper's backpack and pulled out a piece of paper.

"The map!" Opal gasped.

Jasper had the magical map that his parents had made – the map that would tell them where the magical Treasures of Lemuria had been hidden. But now Goldie had it instead, and Loot pecked at it, too.

"Stop that!" Jasper cried.

"Arrrgh," Pegleg squawked anxiously.

"He says they're under some sort of spell," said Opal, lunging forward to try and snatch the map from the parrots' beaks. But she was too late.

Goldie and Loot flew up into the air, taking the magical map with them.

The girls all watched as the birds flew away.

"How will we find the Purple Isle's Treasure now?" Pearl wondered aloud.

And without the Treasure, Opal thought, *how will we break the animals' curse?*

Chapter 4

"The map's gone," said Pearl, her pigtails drooping.

"Mum and Dad," squawked Pegleg sadly.

"And my parents, too," sighed Jasper.

Opal thought for a moment. "The last two gemstones we found were near the palaces. Perhaps if we go to the Purple Isle's palace, we'll find the gemstone there."

"It's as good a place to start as any," said Topaz.

"I know the way," said Thunder. Opal gratefully petted the back of his neck and translated for the others.

They tied Nestor to a small jetty and set off through the thick trees and undergrowth. Vines swung low, wrapping themselves around the friends as they walked. Opal wondered if that was part of the curse.

Thunder's voice sounded far away and wistful as he pushed past a thick frond. "My family have been companions to the royal family for many generations. Every member of the royal household was paired with a panther for protection and companionship. I was supposed to be yours, Opal."

"I guess Obsidian robbed us both of our destinies," Opal replied.

"And our families. My parents died on that ship as well," said Thunder. "I'll never forgive Obsidian for killing my family and ruining this kingdom. When your parents hid the Treasure,

Opal

The Monstrous Forest

the animals slowly started changing. And the people changed, too – they forgot we used to be friends, and treated us as enemies." Thunder sighed sadly. "When Obsidian arrived on the Purple Isle looking for the magical Treasure, I ran. But she caught me."

Opal wrapped her arms around Thunder's neck and squeezed him tightly. "I'm so glad we've found each other now."

Thunder purred and rubbed up against her. "Me too," he said, closing his eyes.

Opal looked up to see the other girls standing around watching them. They hadn't understood Thunder's words, but the emotion must have been clear. Coral sniffed back a tear and Jade blinked. Topaz and Pearl looked at the ground.

"How about we stop here for a short rest?" Topaz suggested, her voice croaky as if she was trying not to cry. "I'm thirsty."

They were standing by a beautiful clearing where exotic, colourful flowers surrounded a clear blue pool. "Good idea," said Opal.

Topaz raced forward and knelt by the side of the pool while Opal gazed around. She'd never seen plants like these before: fat, purple hanging flowers, with stamens that looked like golden balls. She touched one with her finger and it made a noise like a tinkling bell. Opal smiled.

Topaz cupped her hands and splashed water into her mouth. Pearl raced over and sat beside her, doing the same, scooping handful after handful of water down her throat.

"It tastes delicious!" said Pearl. "Like raspberry juice. My favourite."

"No it doesn't," said Topaz, "it tastes like blackcurrant cordial. *My* favourite."

Opal wanted to taste the amazing water, but a rustling in the trees made her stop. Thunder sniffed the air. "More animals are coming this way," he said. "We'd better get going."

Thunder was right. If the animals here were anything like the ones by the river then they should be avoided.

"Topaz?" said Opal.

Topaz snapped her head up from the pool and scowled at her. "What?"

"Don't you think we'd better ...?" Opal thumbed in the direction they'd been heading.

Topaz sighed and hauled herself up. "I suppose so. Come on then."

They set off again, pushing through the forest.

"This place is so boring," said Pearl.

Opal frowned. That hurt. This was *her* island and she thought it was anything but boring.

"What's wrong?" Jade asked her.

"Why can't we go to another island?" Pearl whined. "Like one with more water. I can't turn into a mermaid here."

"Oh, stop moaning," said Topaz. "It's really annoying!"

Opal and Jade exchanged shocked glances. Opal didn't like to hear bad things being said about her island, and she wouldn't have been as harsh as Topaz had been. "I sympathise, Pearl," Opal told her. "It looks like none of the animals understand me here, so ..."

"Oh great, so we're both useless!" Pearl rolled her eyes.

That hurt Opal even more. Coral put a hand on her shoulder.

Suddenly Topaz drew her cutlass.

"Did you hear something?" Jade asked her.

"No," said Topaz. "I just realised that we'd move a lot quicker without all these stupid plants in the way. I wish we had a bulldozer. But at least I can ..." She was about to swing her cutlass across a beautiful bush, but Opal grabbed her arm before she could.

"No one is hacking at this forest or bulldozing anything," she told Topaz firmly. "We're not going to destroy the environment just because it's a little inconvenient."

Topaz rolled her eyes just as Pearl had. "Fine," she said, but the way she said it made it sound anything but fine.

Opal dropped Topaz's arm warily, not trusting that she wouldn't take another swipe when she wasn't looking. Jade and Coral exchanged looks.

"What's got into them?" Jasper asked, craning forward to talk to Opal. "Are they usually this grumpy?"

Opal shook her head. "Never." She'd known Topaz and Pearl almost all her life – they were like sisters to her – and this attitude was most definitely not normal.

A while later Thunder stopped again. "I smell something," he said. "It smells like ... people."

Opal grinned. "My people!" she said. If they were still living on the island, maybe they could shed some light on what had happened. "Where are they?"

Thunder sniffed. "This way!" he replied.

Opal told the others what Thunder had said and they followed him. The panther kept his nose low to the ground until they reached a sheer rockface.

"Dead end?" asked Jade.

Opal touched the rock. "I don't think so ..." She ran her fingers all over it. There were cracks at one side of the rock face. "I think it's a cave!" she said. "Topaz, can you shift this?"

Topaz crossed her arms and tapped her fingers. "Do I have to do everything?"

"Too heavy for you?" Pearl sneered at her.

"That's not what I said, is it?" Topaz snapped back. She bent down and pushed her fingers under the rock, shifting it to one side.

Opal thanked her, but Topaz didn't reply. *What was up with Topaz and Pearl?*

But Opal couldn't worry about her friends now. Racing into the cave, she was thrilled to see burning torches on the walls. The floor was

carpeted with branches, bracken and moss, laid out with paths to walk on.

"There are definitely people living here!" Coral called.

Opal wondered if the people on her island would recognise her straight away, and whether they would look like her – dark-skinned with black hair and amber eyes.

"Hello?" said Jade.

The friends turned a corner, and then skidded to a halt as they came face-to-face with a group of people holding sticks and rusty weapons.

"Retreat! Retreat!" squawked Pegleg.

Topaz drew her cutlass again. "So it's a fight you want, is it?"

"Topaz, no!" Opal told her.

A man with a dark, stubbly face stepped forward. "Get out!" he shouted. "Our cave can't hold any more."

A woman stepped forward and poked Thunder with her stick. "And we don't allow any animals in here."

Coral tugged on Opal's arm. "Opal," she whispered. "Tell them who you are!"

Opal opened her mouth to speak. Her heart pounded in her chest. She needed to tell these people they were the princesses, the saviours of Lemuria. She should say that they'd come to help and stop Obsidian once and for all ... but instead her mouth flapped open and shut like a mechanical toy gone berserk.

The people in the caves narrowed their eyes at them. "Are you working for Obsidian?" the man demanded.

Opal's face started getting hot. Everyone was looking at her.

Topaz huffed and rolled her eyes.

"Hopeless," muttered Pearl under her breath.

Jade cleared her throat and stepped forward.
"We're ... erm ... the princesses," she told the
people. "I'm Jade. This is Coral, Topaz and
Pearl. And this is Princess Opal – the princess
of your Purple Isle." She pushed Opal forward.
Opal stumbled a little.

"Sorry," Jade
whispered.

All eyes
were on Opal
again. "I ...
I ... I ..." but she
couldn't speak a word.

The woman shook
her head. "You hardly
seem like the saviours
Celestine promised us," she said, cocking her
head to the side. "Whoever you are, I suggest you

leave the way you came."

Another woman stepped up beside her. "You must get off this island. It's a very bad place."

Opal's friends continued to stare at her, urging her to say something to convince these people that she was their rightful princess, but Opal couldn't. Instead she turned to them. "Perhaps we should just go," she said. "Once we find the gemstone we'll be able to put everything right."

"I'm the captain here," said Topaz. "I'm the one who says if we should leave."

"Has anyone seen my parents?" Jasper called out. "They're map-makers. My dad looks a bit like me, messy hair, always with a pencil behind his ear. My mum has my same hair colour and the same grin." He forced a smile now. "Or so I'm told."

"I don't care who you are," the man said.

"Just get out."

Jasper and the girls turned and headed out of the cave the way they came.

"Well, that was a waste of time," said Pearl.

"Let's go and drink more water from that pool," suggested Topaz.

A thought suddenly struck Opal: *Topaz and Pearl had started acting mean after they drank from the pool. Had the water done something to them?*

With a shock, Opal now saw that both Pearl's and Topaz's eyes were slightly pink. She remembered the terrifying blood-red eyes of the monkey who'd attacked them earlier.

Were her friends falling under the same curse that had transformed the animals on the island into monsters? If so, how long would it be before her friends became monsters, too?

Chapter 5

Thunder led the way towards the palace.

"I'm sorry we haven't found your parents yet," Opal said to Jasper as they walked. "Once the island is fixed, we can ask Pegleg's parents where they are."

"But we can't fix the island without finding the Treasure," said Jade.

"And we can't find the Treasure without finding the map," added Coral.

"And we can't find the map without speaking to Pegleg's parents," said Opal.

"And we can't speak to Pegleg's parents without finding the Treasure," said Jasper.

What a hopeless situation! Opal's feet felt very heavy as they trudged through the forest.

Finally, Thunder stopped in front of a tree with low-hanging branches.

"Are we taking another break?" asked Coral, eyebrows raised hopefully.

Thunder shook his head. "Princess Opal," he said. "Why don't you push back that branch?"

Opal did as Thunder suggested, and found herself looking down into a valley. In the middle of the valley was the biggest tree she'd ever seen. Its trunk was as wide and tall as a skyscraper, with windows, doors, balconies and walkways built in and around it. The walkways and ladders were made from wood and vines. Wooden houses surrounded the foot of the tree like overgrown toadstools, paths snaking between them. Each roof had a funnel of leaves to collect rainwater, and rope vines acted on levers and pulleys to work lifts and drawbridges. Everything was wooden and natural, all the structures blending into nature.

"This island is amazing," said Jade. "The people that lived here must have been very clever to build it all. I'd love to find out how they did it!"

Opal smiled, despite the situation. What a fantastic place her island was! "And is that ...?" she said, pointing to the tree in the centre.

Thunder nodded. "That's the palace where you and I were born."

"Isn't it amazing?" Opal said to her friends.

While Jade and Coral nodded in agreement, Topaz sneered. "I don't know," she said, "it's a bit ... tree-y."

Opal stepped into the valley and motioned to her friends. "Come on," she said. "Follow me."

Opal
The Monstrous Forest

The girls, Jasper and Thunder ran down the valley through the houses until they reached the central tree of the palace. Opal found a ladder and started climbing towards a balcony. When she got to the top, she turned to offer Topaz a hand.

"I don't need help," said Topaz, whacking her hand away. "I'm stronger than you." Then she leapt over the last three rungs of the ladder and on to the balcony in a single bound.

The walkway up to the palace entrance wound around the tree like a helter-skelter. Branches and vines hung down to cover the walkway, shading it from the sun and rain. Opal was impressed, until one of the vines tried to grab her. "Look out!" she yelled, jumping out of the way.

Another vine wrapped itself around Jade's arm. "Get it off me!" Jade screamed.

Thunder sank his teeth into the vine and it

pulled away.

"It's like the vines have minds of their own," said Opal.

"I'm not sure they like us," added Coral.

Opal turned to see that the vines had now meshed themselves together like a cobweb blocking the whole of the walkway.

"Hey!" yelled Jade. She ran forward to push the vines out of the way, but they instantly reached out to grab her as soon as she approached. "What do we do?" she

asked the others.

"Some princess you are," muttered Pearl.

"Could we cut them down?" suggested Jasper.

Opal thought about this for a moment. They did have Topaz's cutlass, but she didn't like the idea of hurting a living thing ... even if it was a plant that was out to get them! She shook her head. "There must be another way."

Opal looked around her. Her friends had so many powers, there must be something one of them could do. Her eyes landed on Topaz, who was examining her nails.

"Topaz," she said, "do you think you'd be able to hold up these vines so we could get underneath, please? You're the only one of us strong enough to do it."

Topaz rolled her eyes. "I *would* be able to, of course," she said. And then she sighed. "But I don't want to."

"Topaz!" Coral gasped.

"Are you saying you won't help us?" Opal said, not quite able to believe how horrible Topaz was being.

"That's exactly what I'm saying," said Topaz. "I won't help you, so you're stuck!"

Topaz grinned, showing her teeth – all of them now pointed into fangs. The curse had got her!

If Opal couldn't rely on her friends' help, she didn't know what she'd do. They needed to work together if they were going to save her island. But it looked like Topaz and Pearl were losing who they really were. They were becoming monsters!

Coral, Jade and Jasper were all open-mouthed listening to how rude Topaz was being, while Pearl giggled into her hand, clearly loving every minute.

"I'm sick of climbing," moaned Topaz, and she folded her arms in front of her chest. "I'm sick of this island, too. It's stupid. The people are rude and the animals are crazy and I'm done with it."

"They're only crazy because they've drunk the water," said Coral. "You've gone a little crazy too, FYI."

Topaz whipped around and bared her teeth at Coral. "Shut up!" she snapped. "I'm leaving. I'm going back to my island. Then I'll be in charge and everyone will do as I say."

Opal frowned hard. This was so unlike Topaz. She was the captain of their ship and always looked out for her crewmates. Opal stared at her friend, trying to find the real Topaz behind the red eyes. Her hair, which was normally thick and curly, now hung in dank strings. Opal had always felt reassured that Topaz was in charge. But this was her island, and now it was up to her. She was going to have to be confident for once.

Opal took a deep breath and tried to sound firm. "Topaz," she said, "you've forgotten who you are. You're being rude, and you're not acting like the captain you should be. You've always told us that a captain is only as strong as her team ... well, a team is only as strong as their captain, and right now you're being weak!"

Pearl giggled again.

Opal turned and glared at her. "That goes for you too, Pearl!" Opal realised she was starting to sound like their headmistress, Miss Whitestone. It gave her strength to continue. "Topaz, hold up those vines so we can get through and save my island."

There was a moment of wide-eyed quiet as Jasper, Jade and Coral waited to see how Topaz would react. Pegleg hid his head behind a wing, and even Thunder flattened his ears.

Topaz finally sighed and rolled her eyes. "Fine," she huffed, walking towards the vines. One tried to grab her but she batted it away and it shrank back. Then Topaz bent down and lifted up the wall of vines as if it were a heavy curtain and not a writhing, monstrous creature out to get her.

"Get a move on then," she said to the others, holding the vines above her head.

Opal scurried under, thanking Topaz as she went. Jade followed close behind and patted Opal on the back. "Well done, Opal," she said. "I don't think I'd have been brave enough to speak to Topaz like that!"

"Yeah," said Jasper. "You were really confident."

"Must be your royal blood coming through," added Coral.

Opal had never been called brave or confident in her life! But it turned out, when she really needed to, she could rise to the challenge.

Pearl ducked under the vines followed by Pegleg and Topaz, clearly sulking. But it didn't matter – they'd done it. And the palace entrance was just up ahead!

Chapter 6

The walkway led to an open balcony and two doors. Jade pulled a rope and the doors swung open. Opal held her breath – this was her palace, her home. They walked under the archway and into a grand entrance hall inside the tree. Everything in the hall was wooden and carved into intricate designs.

"It's just like I remember it," breathed Thunder. "Only far fewer people, of course."

Light came in through another archway in front of them, which led out to a further balcony on the other side of the tree trunk.

The large hall was lit by torches that held flickering blue stones. Opal grabbed a torch and held it close to the carvings on the wall, to see a picture so detailed it could have been a photograph. It showed a bald man with a beard, and a woman with her hair in intricately knotted braids that reached to her waist. Both had crowns on their heads, and the woman held a baby whose eyes glittered as Opal moved the torch.

"Your mother looks so like you!" said Coral.

"You're sure that's my mother?" asked Opal. She had hoped it was, but she couldn't allow herself to be certain.

"Of course," said Jade. "Look at the baby she's holding. They've set amber into its eyes. Your eyes are amber-coloured."

Opal felt a lump in her throat. "Is it them, Thunder?"

Opal
The Monstrous Forest

Thunder purred, but there was sadness in his purr too. "Those are your parents," he said. "And those," he nodded at the bottom of the mural, where two beautiful panthers twirled around the legs of the king and queen, "are *my* parents."

Opal moved her blue torch down to the bottom of the mural and saw a little cub sitting by a wicker basket.

"And that's you!" Opal touched her free hand against Thunder's head. Then she looked back at the mural and her parents. Their smiles were so kind and so gentle. She wished she could talk to them.

"I wonder if there's a message from my parents somewhere." Topaz had received one on her island, and Jade had too. Surely her parents had loved her just as much. "I wonder where they would've hidden it."

Thunder bowed his head. "There was a

message," he said. "But it's gone."

Opal put her hand over her mouth.

"What did he say?" asked Coral.

Thunder continued. "You see that locket around my neck?" He motioned to the mural again and Opal could see a locket, set in gold with an amber stone in the centre. It glinted in the torchlight.

"That locket contained a message for you," he said. "They put it there before they set out to sea that day. They knew one day you'd find me."

Opal told the others what Thunder had said.

"So where's the locket now?" asked Jade.

Thunder looked at the floor. "I lost it when I was running from Obsidian," he said. "It could be anywhere on this island. Opal, I'm so, so sorry."

Opal felt sad, but she didn't blame Thunder. "It's not your fault," she told him. "It's that mean, horrible witch! When I get my hands on

Obsidian—"

"Squawk!"

Opal looked at Pegleg. "Was that you?" But the bird shook his head.

"It sounded like it was coming from above us," said Jade, looking up.

She was right. The squawking continued and Opal couldn't understand a word of it. "It must be one of the enchanted animals – it sounds like Pegleg's parents," she said.

"Maybe they still have the map," said Jasper.

Opal raised her torch and the light fell on a spiral staircase in one corner of the hall.

"That way!" pointed Coral.

"I'm not chasing after some random noise," said Pearl huffily. Opal sighed. Pearl would normally be the first to bounce into action.

"Me neither," said Topaz.

Opal realised that it might be better if they

didn't come. All this bickering was just holding them up. "OK," she said. "You two stay here."

"Fine," said Pearl, and she sat down on the wooden floor.

"Suits me," said Topaz, slumping next to her.

The others raced up the spiral staircase that twisted around the inside of the tree. The only light came from the torch Opal held, which cast eerie shadows as they went.

But the stairs led to nowhere. Just a landing with no doors, no windows ... nothing.

"How odd," murmured Jade.

Another squawk came from just above their heads. Opal looked up, holding the torch above her. "A trapdoor!" she gasped.

The squawking suddenly stopped.

Jasper put a finger to his lips.

Jade, Jasper and Coral linked their hands to make a step and boosted Opal up so she could reach the trapdoor. Opal opened it as slowly as she could, wincing a little when it creaked. She peered through the tiny gap – on the other side was a circular wooden lookout, with railings and a telescope. But the floor was covered in straw, twigs, leaves and feathers.

"It's a crow's nest," she whispered.

"Like a crow's nest on a ship or an actual nest for crows?" asked Coral.

"Kind of both," Opal replied.

The nest glinted and glittered with the twinkly light of precious things: silver clockwork watches that looked like they belonged on Jade's island, delicate silks like the ones they'd seen on Topaz's island, jewellery, gemstones – none the right colour to be the Treasure they were looking for. Just out of arm's reach was a beautiful gold locket with an amber stone.

"Thunder! The locket!" she cried. Then she clapped her hand over her mouth.

Above her, she heard the birds' squawks become panicked. Two parrot heads peeked over the trapdoor so they were face-to-face with Opal. "Goldie and Loot!" cried Opal, and Loot dropped the map she held in her beak.

"Mum! Dad!" Pegleg cried, flapping up to see them.

Opal opened the trapdoor, hoping Pegleg

could talk some sense into his parents, but they just cawed furiously, snapping at him with their sharp beaks.

As Pegleg kept on squawking, trying to reason with Goldie and Loot, Opal stretched forward to grab the map. She was almost there, her fingertips just touching the edge of it!

"Ow!" A sharp claw pinned Opal's hand down. It was Goldie, his talon digging into her flesh. It really hurt! "Let me go!" Opal cried.

Pegleg flapped around his father, shouting at him to let go.

Then there was an almighty roar and Thunder leapt up. His paw made it through the trapdoor and he swiped at the birds. They flew into the air, terrified.

Opal's hand bled a little from the scratch, but she ignored that, reaching forward and grabbing the map and the locket. "Got 'em!"

Her friends lowered her slowly back down, their muscles aching from the effort of holding her. Pegleg flew back through the trapdoor before it shut. Opal turned to her friends and waved the map and the locket in front of them.

"The map!" cried Jasper.

"You found it," smiled Coral.

"What's that?" asked Jade, pointing to the locket.

Opal squeezed the golden necklace tight.

"A message from my parents," she said. "I hope!"

Chapter 7

Opal took a deep breath and opened the locket. A piece of paper fluttered out, and she grabbed it and unfolded it.

Dear Opal,

Our darling girl, the light of our lives. We're so sorry we can't be with you.

But, if you're reading this, then you have found your companion, Thunder, and you're together again. He will look after you, just as we would have. He's your family now.

You must have the courage to be brave and stand up for what you believe in. Not just against Obsidian, but against any wrong that needs to be righted. Have faith in your feelings. Do not be afraid to speak out. In this way, you will make a fabulous ruler. Please continue our legacy of peace between humans and animals. That is the ethos of this wonderful island.

Gain strength from our love forever.

Your adoring parents.

Opal took a deep breath. Strangely, she didn't feel like crying any more. She felt ready to take on anything. She was the ruler of this island and it was up to her to fix it.

"Hand me the map," Opal said to her friends.

As soon as she held it, both her opal ring and the map began to glow. But rather than an X marking the spot on the map, a long glowing line appeared.

"That's never happened before," Jade exclaimed.

"It's like it's showing us the path from here to the Treasure!" said Jasper.

"Your parents are the coolest," Coral told Jasper.

"I know." Jasper smiled sadly. "I hope one day you'll get to see just how cool they are."

Opal touched the glowing line. The area enlarged as if the map was a computer screen and not parchment.

"The line starts right there," she said, pointing to the other side of the room where the wooden wall was covered by a curtain of vines. At least these ones didn't try to grab them! Opal walked over to the vines and pulled them aside. There, hidden behind them, was another carved mural. Opal had to pull and pull to uncover it all. "It's a flower," she said. The flower was the height of the tall wall. It had large, fat petals which opened up like an orchid.

"It's so pretty," said Coral.

"But it's also pretty terrifying," said Jasper.

Opal had to agree with Jasper. In the centre of the flower there was a mouth, gaping open. The mouth had sharp teeth and a long forked tongue, like a snake's, sticking out. Though the mural was just a carving, it seemed so lifelike.

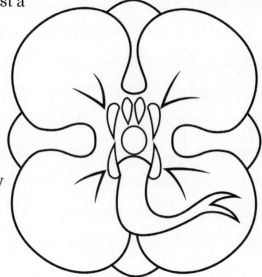

"It's like the flower could bite my hand off!" Opal said to the others.

"Then you're not going to like what I've just noticed," said Jade, wincing. "Look at the centre of the flower again," she said.

There was a hole in the mural. And the hole was a perfect circle, just the size and shape of Opal's ring.

The gemstone Treasures of each island were hidden in a place where no one but the princesses could find them. Only Opal's ring could open this door.

Opal brought her ring forward. "It's perfect," she said, still full of the confidence her parents' letter had given her. "I'll unlock the door ..." She inserted her ring and there was a clicking noise as the mechanism moved. "The door's unlocked ..." she said, flinging the door wide open and taking a big step forward. "And we'll find a perfect pa-a-a-AHH!" Opal made a grab for the doorframe.

Opal

The Monstrous Forest

"Whoa!" Coral lurched forward and grabbed Opal around the waist.

Jasper and Jade took Opal's arms.

There was no perfect path – there was no path at all! There was just a sheer drop down the trunk of the tree. Opal could see the tops of the houses and the smaller trees far below.

Her friends pulled her back into the room.

Opal caught her breath, her heart beating wildly. "Errr, thanks," she said. "That was close."

"Why would there be a door that leads to nothing?" said Jasper, studying the map and the treetops again.

"Does the map want us to fall to our deaths?" asked Coral.

While her friends were looking down at the massive drop below, Opal glanced up. "I've got it!" she cried.

From the top of the door stretched a long

wire that disappeared into the trees. Looking at the map again, she saw that the line followed the same direction as the wire.

"I think we're supposed to go this way," she told the others.

Coral and Jade looked at the wire and grinned. "Cool!" They said together.

"I love zip-wiring," Jade added, "but this is by far the highest I've ever seen."

Opal had to admit it looked fun. They'd gone on a zip wire a couple of years ago with the school and had a great time. But, as Opal looked at the T-bars they were supposed to hold on to, she saw there were no harnesses.

"Think we can hold on?" she said to the others, handing them a T-bar each.

"Easy-peasy," said Jade.

The sounds of Topaz and Pearl arguing floated up the stairs.

"Pearl is a much better gemstone than topaz," Pearl was saying. "You pick it straight out of the sea."

Topaz scoffed. "Pearls are boring white," she said. "Topaz is a pretty honey colour."

"What do we do about Tweedlegrump and Tweedleangry?" asked Coral, pointing at the stairs.

Opal frowned. Topaz and Pearl were holding them up with all their arguing. And they were certainly no help. "They'll just get worse and worse until we find the gemstone," said Opal.

"So we're going to leave them?" said Jade, shaking her head.

"What if they wander off?" asked Coral. "How will we find them?"

Opal thought about their motto: all friends on deck. She knew they should stick together, but wasn't finding the gemstone and saving the island and its inhabitants – humans and animals – more important?

"I'll stay with them," offered Jasper.

Opal hugged him. "Thank you so much," she said. "We really appreciate it."

"It's what my parents would have wanted me to do," he said. Then he took a deep breath as if to steady his nerves, and slowly descended the stairs with Pegleg on his shoulder.

"Oh look," the girls heard Topaz say, "it's the parrot without a leg."

"And the boy without a comb," added Pearl.

Coral hid a giggle behind her hand. "Poor Jasper and Pegleg," she said.

"Give me a zip wire over Monster Topaz and Monster Pearl any day," said Jade.

Opal took a deep breath and grabbed a T-bar. "I'm going first," she said.

Thunder growled. "I don't think so," he said.

"We don't know where the zip wire leads. It might not be safe."

"This is my island and I need to protect it," Opal told him firmly. "Someone has to go first. It should be me."

Thunder bowed his head. "As you command, Your Highness."

Coral grinned at Opal. "You sounded like a proper princess, Opal."

"Yeah," said Jade nodding, impressed. "Go Opal!"

Opal took the T-bar again and stepped out of the door. "Then this princess is going to take flight!" she said, swallowing heavily. Looking at the canopy below she couldn't help but feel nervous. "Here goes!"

Opal stepped out into thin air. Her arms strained as they took the weight of her body, and she held on tightly as she sped through the air.

"See you on the other side!" she called as she flew.

The zip wire travelled through the tops of trees, leaves brushing her hair and skin as she passed by, but never hurting her. She saw intricate nests, some of which looked more like man-made, man-sized huts than birds' nests! The animals here were clearly very large and very skilful. Flowers and fruits of all different colours flew past.

From here she could see so much of her island: the forests and rivers they'd passed by earlier, but also vast green grassy plains dotted with herds of elephants. Opal noticed the elephants had six sharp tusks, and they roared and reared up at each other. Opal knew that their rage was because of the missing gemstone. Once it was found, and Opal sat on the throne, everything would right itself.

The zip wire descended, and as she got closer to the ground she whizzed along even faster than before. She let out a loud, "Wheeeeee!" This was the best ride she'd ever been on!

Opal could now see where the zip wire ended. Just before it was a deep carpet of dead leaves. *As good as any crash mat,* she hoped. Tucking up her legs, she let go of the T-bar, and dropped. Opal landed comfortably and lay back in the leaves, enjoying the way the adrenalin made her head buzz. But then she heard a cry. "Look out!" shrieked Coral as she came whizzing down and landed on the leaves beside her. Thunder followed in a kind of harness made of vines, and Jade came last. She must have made the harness for Thunder.

"That," said Coral, jumping up and dusting the leaves off her skirt and waistcoat, "was completely brilliant." Jade adjusted her hat.

"Awesome!"

Just then they heard a pathetic mew.

"Poor kitty," said Coral, undoing Thunder's harness.

Thunder shook himself as if he was shaking off rainwater. Opal heard him mutter, "Cats aren't meant to fly."

Opal looked at the map again. The Treasure didn't look too far away now. The foliage was even thicker than the forest they'd walked through before, but Opal led the way. She pushed back vines, climbed over fallen logs and jumped over the deep puddles that dotted the path. Clearly, no one had travelled this way in years.

"It should be just ... through ... here ..." she said to her friends. Opal hoped that she would see the gemstone of her island, probably a large opal. But instead she came face-to-face with a bubbling black swamp.

"What's that smell?" said Coral, appearing beside her.

The swamp smelt like month-old bins. Opal held her nose.

"I wish I could hold *my* nose," Thunder whined.

"Look at that!" Jade exclaimed, pointing ahead.

In the centre of the swamp was a huge flower – the exact one that they'd seen on the mural. Its petals were open, but they were blood-red, throbbing and pulsating. There was a snarling sound and Opal started backwards – the flower had growled at them! The mouth in the middle of the flower opened and shut. Saliva dripped from each pointed tooth. The friends huddled together and Thunder pressed himself against Opal's legs.

"That's bad news," said Coral.

Opal glanced back down at the map. "You think that's bad news," she told her friends. "I think I know where the gemstone is ..."

Thunder and the girls looked at her

expectantly.

"Inside that flower!" she gulped.

Coral turned pale and Jade closed her eyes in fear. Thunder whined again.

They'd found the gemstone. But they had no way of getting it!

Chapter 8

Picking up the gemstone without losing an arm was going to be a challenge. And the plant was in the middle of a swamp. How would they even get to it?

"What do we ...?" Opal started to say, but when she looked at Jade and Coral she could tell they had no idea. Opal took a deep breath. It was up to her.

"It's just a plant," said Opal. "The four of us can outsmart a plant!"

The plant snapped and growled angrily as if it

had understood.

"No offence," Opal told it. "Coral, this swamp is just muddy water. Can you do something with it?"

Coral grinned. "I certainly can." She stepped to the edge of the swamp, held out her arms, then raised them slowly. Water rose to the surface of the swamp, then flew up through the air like raindrops in reverse.

Opal wasn't sure what Coral was doing until she saw that, as the water lifted from the swamp, the mud began to harden.

Opal stepped on to the swamp, finding the mud as solid as concrete. "We can walk right over it!" she said. It was slippery though, so they had to go slowly.

Jade, Coral and Thunder walked carefully beside her. The monstrous flower, sensing them approaching, snapped and growled harder and louder. As its mouth opened, Opal saw something glinting inside. Something purple with multicoloured flecks. "There it is!" she cried. "The gemstone."

"That's great," said Coral. "But how do we get it out? We need to distract the flower."

"Leave it to me," said Jade. She had *that* look on her face and Opal knew she was inventing something.

Opal and Coral squeezed each other's hands tight. "I love it when Jade goes into inventor mode," Coral whispered.

Jade took out some tools from her tool belt. She started working on something in her hands. "See that vine?" she said, pointing but not looking up.

The vine she was pointing at was dangling from a tall tree.

"Tug it," Jade instructed. "Will it take a decent

amount of weight?"

Thunder pulled at it with his teeth and it didn't break.

"Good. Now grab some branches – thick ones."

Opal and Coral did as they were told. Opal might be princess of this island, but when it came to inventing, Jade was in charge.

There were more instructions: grab this, tie that, pass me that – but it was only when Jade handed Opal the end of the vine that Opal saw what she had created.

"Now ... pull," said Jade.

Opal pulled the vine and a wooden creature swung towards them. It had a body made of a thick log, and jaws made of snapping branches. It even had leafy wings! Coral had to duck to avoid being hit, but by pulling the various vines they could move the wooden creature, just like a puppet. Opal pulled a vine that made the creature's mouth open and shut like an alligator's. Thunder growled, impressed.

"Good work, Jade!" said Opal. "Now let's see if it'll be enough to distract the monster plant."

Together, they used the vines to angle the beast towards the flower, but it saw them and turned, opening its petals wide to attack. Opal glimpsed the gemstone deep inside the mouth.

This was it. She had to be brave. Opal handed her vine to Coral and crept towards the flower. Her heart pounded as she tiptoed closer and closer.

The plant tried to snap its sharp teeth around the wooden contraption. But the log body was too big for the plant's jaws and stuck in its mouth, wedging it open.

Opal leapt forward and reached in, careful not to scratch her arm on the sharp teeth. The plant roared, enraged. Opal's fingertips touched the gemstone. It was cool and smooth. She snatched it out, just as the log broke in two and the plant's jaws slammed shut, teeth closing just where her arm had been half a second before. Opal fell back on to her bottom and opened her hand to reveal the island's Treasure – the beautiful multicoloured gemstone. It was purple, but sprinkled with every colour imaginable. Just like her ring, it was like looking into the universe.

"We got it!" Opal cried, holding it aloft.

Jade and Coral clapped their hands in delight. "Now we just need to get you to the throne," said Coral.

The magic would only work once Opal was holding the gemstone while sitting on the throne.

"But where is the throne?" asked Jade. "We never saw one at the palace."

Thunder growled. "I don't remember there being a throne in the palace."

"Thrones are always in palaces," said Coral.

Normally Opal would agree, but she got the

impression that her people were more into the outdoors than the indoors. The throne could be anywhere!

Opal's friends pulled her off the ground, but then she saw their eyes fix on something behind her. She turned to see that something was happening to the plant.

"I hope I didn't hurt it," said Opal. The plant had tried to hurt her, but that wasn't its fault.

The petals of the plant opened out wider than before. The mouth in the centre of the flower closed and puffed out like a pillow. The top petals bunched together to form an umbrella above, while the bottom petals became a seat.

"Do you think ...?" said Coral.

"It couldn't be ..." said Jade.

"That's the throne!" said Thunder.

It made perfect sense to Opal.

"Well, what are you waiting for?" asked Jade.

Excitement bubbled up inside Opal. She took the Treasure in both hands and crept towards the plant that had tried to eat her, then sat gingerly on the petal seat. The second she did so, the gemstone disappeared from her hands. She felt something on her head and knew what it was: the crown of the Purple Isle! Coral and Jade beamed at her, and Thunder purred loudly and lay down by her feet.

Opal sat, enjoying the moment, but it wasn't long before curiosity got the better of her and she removed the crown to look at it: a perfect golden crown with the purple gemstone in its centre.

Tears welled up in her eyes. "We did it," she said, hardly able to get the words out. "We've saved my island."

There were squawks and shrieks from above. Opal looked up to see monkeys swinging through the trees and beautiful birds of paradise flying towards them. The animals surrounded the friends, but Opal wasn't scared.

"Are you ... better now?" Opal called up to them.

"Princess Opal!" they called in response. Opal could understand them!

"You've returned!"

"You've saved us!"

Opal's heart swelled. It had worked. She'd broken the hideous curse.

A great trumpeting noise filled the air and the herd of six-tusked elephants Opal had seen earlier lumbered into the swamp, leaving a path through the bushes behind them. The elephants kneeled and bowed their heads. "All hail Princess Opal, and the saviours of Lemuria," they bellowed.

Jade and Coral watched, open-mouthed. "Whoa," Coral breathed.

Behind the elephants, a nervous-looking woman peered out from the trees. Then more and more people joined her, following the path the elephants had made. It was the people from the cave! They looked a lot less angry now. They gathered in front of Opal on her throne and bowed.

"We're sorry, Your Highness," said the man they'd met before.

"We should have believed you when you said

you were the princesses," said the woman who'd poked Thunder with the stick. "I'm sorry," she told the panther.

"It's all right," Opal told them. "How were you supposed to believe me when I couldn't get the words out? I was too scared to act like a princess. I'm going to be more confident from now on."

Jade and Coral made their way through the crowd and put their arms around Opal's shoulders.

There was a familar squawk in the air. "Princess Opal! Princess Opal!"

Opal, Jade and Coral looked to the sky. "Pegleg!" Opal called out. Sure enough, a red, blue and yellow parrot burst through the

treetops, swiftly followed by two more parrots: one with an eyepatch, the other with a wooden leg – Goldie and Loot! The redness had gone from their eyes.

"You're back," smiled Coral.

Three more people burst through the bushes. It was Topaz, Pearl and Jasper! Opal, Jade and Coral rushed forward and hugged them tightly.

"We're back, too!" said Topaz. Her eyes were normal again, and her teeth were no longer sharp.

"I'm sorry we were so horrible," said Pearl, cringing. "I can't believe all the mean things we said."

"Can you forgive us?" asked Topaz.

Opal hugged them again. "It wasn't your fault. It was the stupid curse."

"We know you'd never be mean on purpose," said Coral.

Opal turned to Jasper to thank him for

looking after her friends while they were under the curse. But Jasper was searching the crowd of people. The look on his face was anything but happy.

"What's the matter, Jasper?" Opal asked.

Jasper sighed and Opal thought she could see tears in his eyes. "I'm so pleased the Purple Isle is back to normal and Pegleg has his parents." He forced a smile, then sighed and let it drop. "It's just ... I hoped my parents would be here, too. Perhaps they never were."

Loot flapped down and landed on Jasper's shoulder, chirruping excitedly. Goldie landed on his other shoulder and joined in, squawking "X marks the spot!"

Jasper looked at Opal, hope in his eyes. "What did they say, Opal?"

Opal grinned. "They said your parents are here – and they can take us to them!"

Jasper's lower lip began to wobble and Coral took him by the hand.

"Come on," she said. "Let's go and find your mum and dad."

Chapter 9

J asper sniffed back tears and wiped his nose on his sleeve.

"Cheer up!" squawked Loot, rubbing her beak softly against Jasper's face. She and Goldie continued to squawk and chitter, and Opal listened intently while the others waited with bated breath.

"They say Obsidian came to the Purple Isle to look for the Treasure," Opal translated, "but the cursed animals drove her back, so she thought this was the perfect place to maroon the map-makers. She thought the animals would eat them."

"Were my parents eaten?" Jasper asked, panic in his voice. The humans and animals of the Purple Island were gathering around to listen, and they gasped, too.

"No," Opal said, still listening to Loot. "They escaped!"

A cheer rose up from the islanders.

"They made it as far as a rocky outcrop off the coast. Your parents told the parrots to go and find food, but when Goldie and Loot came back inland they were affected by the curse." Loot looked so sad. Opal stroked her beak and asked, "Can you take us to them?"

Goldie's happy cry and hopping dance needed no translation.

"We'd better be quick," said Topaz. "As soon as Obsidian realises we have the Treasure, she'll be back."

"Princess Opal," said an elephant, "if there is anything we can do to help, we'd gladly be of service."

"All the animals would," growled a leopard.

Five monkeys jumped up and down, screeching in agreement.

Opal looked around and saw two huge birds of paradise high up in a tree.

"How about you two?" she called up to them.

The two birds flapped down from their perches and landed in front of the friends. They were as big as horses, with green bodies and long purple tails.

"We'd gladly help," said one.

"It's the least we can do for the princesses who saved us all," said the other.

"Thank you. Do you think you can fly with a passenger?" Opal asked them.

The birds squawked that they could. Opal turned to her friends. "Jasper and I will go with Pegleg, Goldie and Loot to find Jasper's parents. We'll meet you back on Nestor."

The four girls saluted her. "Aye aye, Captain," said Topaz.

Opal shook her head and winked at Topaz. "You're still the captain," she told her, "but I've got this one."

Jasper climbed up on to one of the birds. Opal was about to do the same, but she heard a mew at her side. She gasped as she looked at Thunder. "I'm sorry, my friend," she said, stroking his ears. A lump formed in her throat. "I wish you could come with us. But we need to hide the crown and the gemstone far away from Obsidian. And the place we're going ... well, I don't think I can hide you there, too."

She tried to imagine bringing a panther to her

dorm room.

"That's OK," Thunder said sadly. "I'll look after the Purple Isle until you return."

"And we will return!" she said, burying her face in his neck. "I promise."

Opal gave Thunder a last stroke and mounted the giant bird. She waved at the people, who bowed to her, calling their thanks. She handed

Topaz the crown and the bird of paradise took off with a whoosh. "See you back on Nestor!" called Opal.

Opal held on tight as they soared into the sky. Loot and Goldie led the way, Pegleg flying between them. Jasper flew on his bird beside Opal and she could see his jaw set hard – scared, but determined to find his parents.

They flew over the forests and past the great tree that was her family's palace. There were animals everywhere – hunting, climbing, searching for food. Opal was so glad to see that the island was safe again. And it was so beautiful. She couldn't wait to come back to explore.

They flew over the edge of a cliff which dropped straight down into the sea.

"Oh no," Jasper called from beside her. "It's Obsidian!"

There, just metres from the shore, was

Obsidian's ship, sailing for the Purple Isle.

"Perhaps you should take the gemstone back now," said Jasper.

Opal shook her head. "No way," she said. "We're finding your parents first. I promised."

There was no time to lose! Loot pointed out the rocky island in the distance. It was desolate – just a couple of jagged rocks with a hut on it. As they flew closer, Opal could see that the hut was made out of bits of wood and debris that must have washed up on the shore.

Jasper smiled proudly. "I bet they made that," he said. "I just hope it means they've survived after all this time."

They landed on the jagged rocks, and Opal had never seen anyone move faster than Jasper did as he slid from the bird's back and ran to the hut. "Mum! Dad!" he called, racing to the door and pulling it open.

"Jasper?" said a surprised voice from inside.

"JASPER!" chorused two voices.

Opal watched as a man and a woman ran out of the hut and wrapped themselves around Jasper, sobbing, weeping and kissing him all over his face. Their clothes were patched and shabby, and they looked thin and tired. But all that melted away when they held their son.

Opal hung back a little longer. She tried not to think about her own parents and how she wished she could see them again. As she watched Jasper and his parents embrace, laughing and crying, Opal smiled, happy for her friend. And she knew her parents would be happy for her, too. She'd saved the island and been brave and confident, just as they'd asked her to.

And I will be brave, forever more!

"Mum, Dad," said Jasper. "This is Opal. Princess Opal!"

Jasper's parents gasped and bowed to Opal,
but Opal ran up to them, shaking her head.

"Oh no," she said. "You two don't have to bow
to anyone. It's your magical map that's helped

us find the Treasures and save Lemuria. All our victories are because of you!"

"I don't know about that," said Jasper's mum. She had the same grin as Jasper. "But can we at least thank you for bringing our son back to us?"

Opal smiled. "Of course," she said. "Let me take you to my friends."

Jasper's mum climbed on to one of the birds of paradise with Opal, while Jasper's dad went with Jasper on the other. Pegleg, Loot and Goldie flew in circles around them. Opal grinned as they flew. This family was back together again.

As they passed Obsidian's ship, Opal asked the birds to swoop down low.

"Hello down there!" she called to Obsidian.

Obsidian looked up, saw Opal and Jasper and his parents, and screamed in wild rage. "I'll get you!" she shouted, shaking her fist.

"Good luck with that!" Opal called back with a

chuckle.

They flew a little further, towards the inlet where they'd left Nestor. And there he was, rocking gently on the blue water. Opal directed the birds to land on the ship. As soon as they touched down on the deck, Jade, Pearl, Coral and Topaz ran to greet them.

"Jasper! Are these your parents?" asked Coral.

"The very same," said Jasper's dad, bowing low to all the princesses.

"We've wanted to meet you for so long," said Pearl.

"Jasper said you were very cool," said Jade.

"They are!" Jasper beamed proudly. His parents laughed and his dad even blushed.

Opal wished she could have stayed longer, talking to Jasper's parents, looking at the beautiful Purple Isle she came from, but with Obsidian so close by she only had one thought on her mind.

"We'd better go," she said to the others. "We need to hide the Treasure. But we'll be back soon for the other gemstones."

"And when we have them," said Jade, "we'll make Obsidian pay for what she's done."

"Nestor!" Opal called out. "When we're gone, will you take Jasper and his family anywhere they want to go, please?"

"Of course" said Nestor. "You know me, always happy to oblige."

Opal shared a grin with her friends. Nestor wasn't

always obliging, but they knew he'd look after this magical map-making family. The girls said goodbye to Jasper and his parents, thanked the birds for their help, and then huddled together.

"Ring bump!" said Opal.

They brought their hands together, and in a flash of golden light, they were gone.

Chapter 10

The golden light faded to be replaced by the harsh fluorescent light of the toilets in the zoo.

"Talk about back to reality," said Coral, as a toilet flushed on the other side of the room.

The girls giggled.

Then Opal remembered why they were here in the first place. She'd been too embarrassed to speak out in front of people from her school. "I feel so silly," she told her friends. "I can't believe I wouldn't speak!"

Her friends gathered around her, shaking

their heads.

"You can be brave enough to tackle a man-eating plant," Jade told her, "but still too scared to talk to a crowd."

"It doesn't make sense," said Coral, "but it's totally normal."

Opal smiled sheepishly at her friends. They were right, but she was determined to be more confident from now on.

"Come on," said Topaz. "Miss Whitestone will start to worry about where we are."

The girls knew that no time passed while they were away in Lemuria, but even so, they'd been in the toilets a while now and they'd better get back. Topaz handed Opal the crown and she put it in her backpack – taking one last look at the sparkling stone at the front. They'd saved the Purple Isle. If she could do that, she could do anything!

They found their class in the reptile house. It was dark inside, the only light coming from the tanks. They passed salamanders, geckos and lizards of all different colours. Opal smiled as she thought that they wouldn't be out of place in the forests of the Purple Isle.

The class listened to the young zookeeper as she reached inside one of the glass tanks. "Here," she said, "is an example of the most famous spider on Earth." Her eyes glinted as she spoke. "And she's my favourite creature in the whole zoo. Her name's Tilly. Tilly the tarantula!"

The girls gasped and some of them stepped back quickly. But not Opal. She pushed through the crowd to get a better look. Her classmates were only too happy to let her by.

"She's beautiful," breathed Opal.

"You think so too?" the zookeeper asked.

Opal nodded. The tarantula might have been

hairy, with eight spindly legs and eight beady eyes, but in her own way, she was beautiful. All animals were.

"Would you like to hold her?" the zookeeper asked.

"Yes please!" Opal said with an excited nod. She reached forward and the zookeeper carefully placed the spider on to her hand. The spider tickled as she walked around Opal's hand and up her arm a little. Opal could hear her classmates gasp and shrink back. One of them shouted "Eww! Gross!" It was Kate.

Opal turned to her. "She's not gross," she said firmly. "Just a little tickly, that's all."

Kate shook her head, but a couple of other girls started to come a little closer. Opal could see that because she wasn't scared of the spider, they weren't either.

"Do you know any cool facts about spiders?"

the zookeeper asked Opal. "Knowing more about Tilly might help everyone like her a little better."

"I do," Opal replied, then she realised the whole group was looking at her again. It scared Opal for a moment, but she pushed her anxiety down. She was a princess pirate! She could speak to these people. "Female spiders like Tilly," Opal said, "can live for up to 30 years."

The zookeeper nodded. "That's right. Tilly here is 25. That's older than me!"

Everyone was still looking, but Opal could see that she had their attention and they were interested in what she had to say. She carried on. "Spiders have eight legs, but if they lose one, like in a battle or something, they can grow another one. Cool, eh?"

Topaz, Pearl and Coral came closer and looked at the tarantula.

"Like a self-building robot!" said Jade with a grin.

Topaz leaned closer so only the girls could hear. "Could be useful for a princess in a battle."

"Her hairs are such cool colours," said Coral. "She's not scary at all!"

Opal gave Tilly back to the zookeeper. She wasn't scared of a spider – even a big spider like Tilly – and she wasn't scared about talking in front of people any more either. She had the confidence she needed, and she could do anything.

At the end of the day the girls trooped to

the coach to take them back to Breakwater Hall. Everyone was giggling and talking about their favourite part of the trip, but Opal's mind was on the crown in her backpack. She couldn't wait to get it back to their room and look at it again.

Opal had stepped on to the coach, following her friends, when Miss Whitestone called her over.

"Did you have a good time today, Opal?"

Opal nodded. "Yes, thank you, Miss Whitestone. I love animals, so this was my perfect school trip."

Miss Whitestone lowered her voice. "I just want you to know that I thought you were very brave today."

Opal raised her eyebrows, remembering how she'd squared up to the man-eating plant, and fought off Obsidian, and spoken to the people of the Purple Isle.

"I know you don't find it easy talking in front of people," Miss Whitestone said.

Opal giggled. Of course that's what Miss Whitestone meant! She thought it was very nice of her to say so.

"You did well," Miss Whitestone went on. "And you were brave to hold the tarantula too! Just imagine if we could understand what that little spider was saying!" she added with a chuckle.

Opal laughed back – if only Miss Whitestone knew! In Lemuria she could speak to all the animals – including her very own panther friend. She couldn't wait to get back there again!

TO BE CONTINUED ...